OWEN DAVEY

PASSIONATE ABOUT
PENGUINS

FLYING EYE BOOKS

King penguins share beaches
with huge elephant seals.

CONTENTS

WHAT ARE PENGUINS?

Penguins are a group of flightless birds that split their time between land and sea. Penguins are chubby, with short legs and wings shaped like flippers. They have dark feathers over their backs and pale ones on their bellies. A group of penguins can be called a "waddle" on land, or a "raft" in the water. Depending on which biologist you ask, there are between seventeen and twenty species of penguin, and these can be split into six distinct groups.

Royal penguin

King penguin

Chinstrap penguin

Humboldt penguin

Yellow-eyed penguin

Little penguin

Crested penguins have red bills, red eyes, and yellow-feathered crests on their heads.

Great penguins are the king penguin and the emperor penguin. They have thin beaks and colorful patches on either side of their head.

Brush-tailed penguins have long tail feathers that sweep the ground as they walk.

Banded penguins are named after the black band on their chest. They also have spots on their bellies and black beaks with a little white mark on them.

The **yellow-eyed penguin** is the only remaining species in this group. It is named after the distinctive coloring around its eyes.

Little penguins have blue-tinged feathers and their scientific name Eudyptula means "good little diver."

Nom Nom

Penguins are carnivores, which means they eat other animals. They hunt in the sea and most commonly prey on fish. Penguins also eat squid, lobsters, crabs, eels, jellyfish, seahorses, and tiny shrimplike creatures called krill.

Home Sweet Home

The "equator" is an imaginary line dividing the north and south of our planet. Nearly all penguins live below the equator, but Galápagos penguins sometimes venture north of it. Some species live as far south as icy Antarctica but penguins live in lots of other habitats, including rocky areas, beaches, and coastal forests. People often imagine penguins and polar bears hanging out together, but they would never meet in the wild. Polar bears only live in the very north of the Earth, known as the "Arctic Circle."

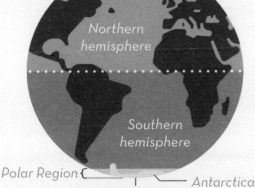

North Pole

Polar Region

Arctic Circle

Northern hemisphere

Equator

Southern hemisphere

Polar Region

Antarctica

South Pole

BY DESIGN

Penguins spend most of their lives in the sea. They are specially adapted to this "aquatic" lifestyle. Take a closer look at some of the features of this Humboldt penguin to see how these birds thrive in our oceans.

Tail

Their short, stiff, wedge-shaped tails can be used to help steer when swimming or balance when walking.

Feet

Their webbed feet are positioned at the back of the body to help with steering and movement in water. The placement of the feet forces penguins to stand in a distinctive upright position on land. Most penguins have three forward-facing toes and one pointing backward. Each toe has a claw for helping penguins to dig or to grip ice and rock when on land.

Black & White Feathers

Having a dark back and light front is an example of "countershading." This helps penguins hide from both predators and prey. If a penguin swims above you, its white belly blends in with the surface of the water, which looks pale from the light of the sun. If a penguin is below you, it is hard to spot its dark back against the ocean below.

Humboldt penguin

Gentoo penguin

Body Shape

While swimming, penguins have an incredibly streamlined shape which tapers at both ends. This helps them move with less effort through water.

Blubber

Penguins have thick layers of fat to help keep them warm, even in freezing-cold waters. This "blubber" can be over an inch thick and can account for a third of a penguin's overall weight.

Wings

The wings are stiff and flat to act like fins. While these are useless for any attempt at flight, they make penguins fast and agile in water. On land, penguins use their wings to help them balance while they walk.

Supraorbital Gland

The ocean has a lot of salt in it, and so does the food penguins eat. Too much salt is bad for them so they use their supraorbital gland to filter excess amounts from their blood. This is excreted as a fluid from their beak.

Penguin wing and bones

Pigeon wing and bones

Bones

Most birds have hollow air-filled bones to help them fly but penguins are designed to sink. Penguins have dense skeletons, which reduces how much they naturally float and makes it easier for them to swim and dive.

Mouth

Penguins don't have teeth: instead they have fleshy spines on their tongues and the inside of their mouths. The spines point toward the back of the throat, which helps them swallow prey.

Eyes

Their eyes are specially adapted for seeing underwater and on land. They rely on their eyesight to find food.

Ears

Penguins have holes for ears. They are on either side of their head and covered by feathers.

Beaks

Hook-shaped beaks help penguins grab and keep hold of slippery sea creatures.

BIRDS OF A FEATHER

The feathers that cover a bird are known collectively as its "plumage." These feathers are made from keratin, just like human hair and fingernails. Feathers have a central shaft, known as a "rachis," and a flat area called a "vane." There are various types of feathers in a penguin's plumage, each with its own look and purpose.

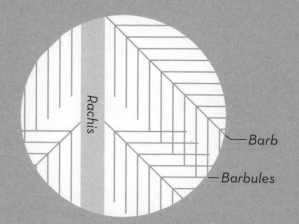

Rachis

— Barb

— Barbules

Quill   Rachis   Vane

Here are some emperor penguin feathers

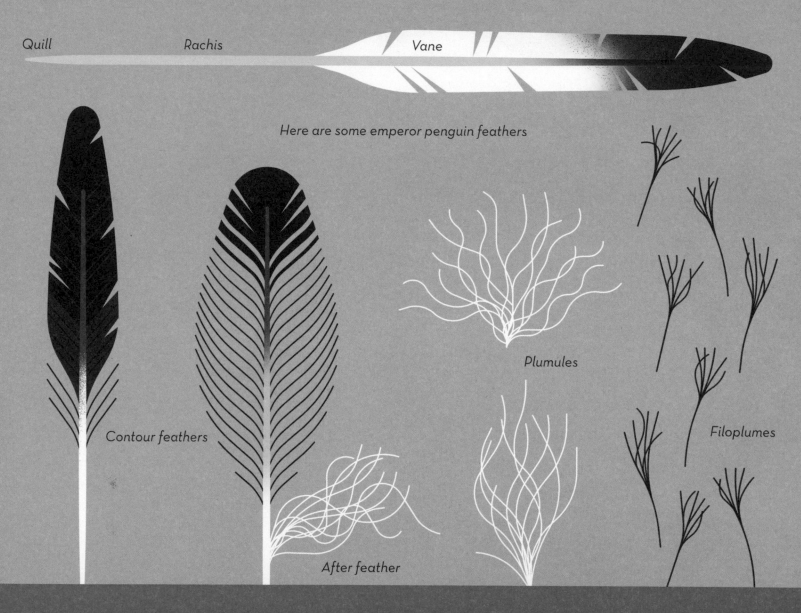

Contour feathers

After feather

Plumules

Filoplumes

Contour feathers are stiff outer feathers that protect the penguin's skin.

After feathers and plumules are soft and fluffy and keep penguins warm. After feathers are attached to the contour feathers.

Penguin plumules are attached directly to the skin. They are more densely packed together than in other birds, which helps to keep them warm in cold conditions.

Filoplumes are very small feathers with a long rachis, short barbs, and barbules at the end.

Move a Muscle

Muscles control the contour feathers to make them stand up on end or flatten against the penguin's body. These outer feathers have lots of barbicels. When laid flat, barbicels lock the barbs together. They act like shingles on the roof of a house to keep water out. They can even trap a layer of air between the skin and the feathers, acting like an built-in blanket.

Preen and Tidy

To work effectively, feathers have to be kept clean and tidy. This is known as "preening." Friends and partners sometimes preen each other, concentrating on the hard-to-reach places, like the head.

All Change

Birds refresh their plumage regularly to keep their feathers in good condition. While most birds lose and regrow feathers gradually, penguins do it all at once. This is called a "catastrophic molt." The new feathers are not yet waterproof, so penguins are stuck on land for the few weeks it takes for them to finish growing. Penguins rely on the sea for food, so they don't eat for this entire time. To help them survive, penguins intentionally eat more before a molt so that they can bulk up and store extra fat in their bodies.

Old feathers

New feathers

This African penguin will lose nearly half its body weight in the three weeks it takes to molt.

GET A MOVE ON

Penguins are designed to be sleek and graceful in the water, but this makes them adorably awkward and clumsy-looking on land. Here are some of the ways penguins get from one place to another.

Waddle Along

Penguins are famous for their funny upright walk. With short legs and plump bodies, they take small steps and sway from side to side, sometimes holding their wings out for balance. Surprisingly, they can waddle along at roughly the same pace as humans and some species can march over 60 miles to reach breeding grounds.

Gentoo penguins trekking along a penguin highway in Antarctica.

Hop To It

Penguins jump with both feet together to move quickly or to cross difficult terrain. Many species can be seen jumping between rocks or skipping over cracked ice.

Eastern rockhopper penguins are named after their excellent jumping abilities.

Let It Slide

Penguins slide along snow and ice on their bellies, using their feet and wings to move and steer. This is called "tobogganing." It is a quick and energy-efficient mode of transport, plus it looks fun.

An emperor penguin tobogganing on its belly.

A little penguin taking a dip.

Going Swimmingly

Penguins are fast swimmers. They use their wings as flippers to move through the water and their tails and feet to change direction. Despite being so adept at moving underwater, they breathe like any other bird. Sooner or later, they have to come back to the surface to grab some air.

What's the Porpoise of This?

A technique called "porpoising" can be used to breathe while swimming. They speed along, constantly jumping in and out of the water, grabbing lungfuls of air as they go. Porpoising is named after the leaping movement porpoises (and dolphins) are famous for. This technique uses a lot of energy so is often reserved for escaping a predator or chasing prey.

The snares penguin travels with speed by using the same swimming technique as porpoises.

THREE SQUARE MEALS

Penguins forage for food in the sea. Some species hunt in the open ocean, known as the "pelagic zone," while others search along the seafloor, called the "benthic zone." Penguins may travel hundreds of miles in search of food. Different types of prey require different hunting techniques and strategies.

Little penguins are following short-tailed shearwaters to find food.

A Bird's Eye View

How do you find food in such a vast ocean? Some studies suggest that penguins look to the skies for help. Seabirds like gannets and gulls hunt small fish and because they fly, they can see larger areas of the ocean at one time. It appears that penguins may sometimes follow these birds to help find food sources.

Gone Fishing

Due to their speed and agility, penguins are more than capable of catching lone fish and swallowing them whole. Penguins dive down and then catch fish from below as they swim back to the surface. Some fish "school" together in a group, making it harder for penguins to target a single fish. Fish at the edge of the school are the most vulnerable and penguins happily pick off any stragglers.

The Galápagos penguin's V-shaped diving path.

African penguins work together to herd the fish into a bait ball.

Take the Bait

Penguins often hunt together, which increases their chances of success. As a small team, they dive around the edges of a school of fish and below it. This forces the fish up to the water's surface and into a panicked, tightly-packed group known as a "bail ball." It is then much easier for the penguins to feed.

In for the Krill

Krill mass together in huge swarms. Penguins simply dart into the middle of this mass, grabbing what krill they can. The swarms are such an important food source in Antarctica that they sustain not only penguins but seals and whales too.

Adélie penguins can eat up to one kilogram of krill every day.

Galápagos penguins forage for food in rocky reefs.

Deep Dive

Some penguins dive down several hundred feet to forage for food in the coastal benthic zone. They can hold their breath for many minutes at a time, targeting prey that will fill their bellies with the least amount of effort.

Some gentoo penguins take a leap of faith.

SELF-DEFENSE

While the sea promises the opportunity of a meal, it also holds danger. Below the surface of the ocean, potential predators lay in wait. Let's look at how penguins survive these treacherous waters.

You First, Buddy

Penguins increase their chances of survival by sticking together. Before entering the water, penguins often gather by ledges overlooking the sea to check if the coast is clear. Sometimes a member of the group grows impatient and dives into the water first. The group watches closely to see what happens to it. If the first bird survives, the rest follow.

Large species like the emperor penguin can leap a foot and a half out of the water, but Adélie penguins can clear ten feet.

Adélie penguin

Emperor penguin

Back on Dry Land

When the water seems too dangerous, getting out is the sensible choice. However, clambering up a steep, rocky ledge or over a layer of sea ice is a near-impossible task for a penguin. Instead, they swim fast to the surface of the water and burst out, getting airborne for just a moment before arriving back on land.

A Turn of Speed

Penguins may be fast swimmers, but the marine animals that prey on them are faster. Penguins try to outmaneuver these larger, less agile creatures by zigzagging with sharp turns, hoping the predator will tire and give up.

Will this orca be able to keep up with this Adélie penguin's tight turns?

This emperor penguin shoots through the water like a torpedo.

Bubble Up

To reach the speed necessary to get airborne, penguins trap air beneath their plumage and dive down into the water. As they swim back up, they release little air bubbles from between their feathers, which coat the penguin. This coat of bubbles makes it easier for the penguin's body to move through water, resulting in their quick aerial exit.

HOT AND COLD

Penguins are the only birds who can breed in climates ranging from 100°F around the equator to -75°F in Antarctica. That's a difference of 175°F! Here is how penguins survive in such extreme conditions.

Out in the Cold

Antarctica is the coldest, driest, windiest continent on our planet. It's so cold that most of it is covered in thick layers of ice and snow all year round. Even in the warmest coastal areas of Antarctica, the temperature is around 32°F. Despite this, these six different penguin species actually breed in Antarctica since their densely packed feathers and fatty blubber keeps them relatively warm in these intensely cold conditions.

King

Gentoo

Chinstrap

Emperor

Macaroni

Adélie

These six species of penguin breed in Antarctica.

Weather the Storm

Adélie penguins can sense when a storm is coming. They lie on the ground in wait, pointing their beaks toward the wind. If they are incubating an egg, however, they simply sit on the nest and tough it out. Penguins will sometimes hold their wings close to their body and shiver to keep themselves warm.

This Adélie penguin knows what's coming.

Current Affairs

Water from the Antarctic is carried as far north as the equator through ocean currents. These cool waters not only bring vital food resources but also help to keep penguins from overheating. There's nothing more refreshing than a cool dip on a warm day, so some penguins simply hunt in the day and come to land in the evening when the sun is less intense.

Keep Your Cool

Penguins can lose heat quickly through areas with fewer or no feathers, like their feet. Some species have areas of bare skin on their faces, known as "heat windows." Penguins also have fewer feathers on their wings. In these areas, penguins have blood vessels very close to each other. This allows penguins to recycle heat within their body, which helps them heat up or cool down.

Galápagos penguins

African penguins have large patches of bare skin around their face.

Southern rockhopper penguins stand with their wings out to help body heat escape.

King penguins try to minimize how much their feet touch the frozen ground by rocking back onto their heels and lifting their toes in the air. Their stiff tails help them stay upright.

Some penguins pant like a dog to stay cool. By holding its mouth open and breathing heavily, some of the moisture in the penguin's body begins to evaporate in the heat.

19

BORN THIS WAY

All birds start life in an egg. Adult penguins come ashore to build nests, lay eggs, and raise their chicks. Some choose rocky coasts and islands, while others head to more secluded locations inland to protect their eggs from predators.

Nesting

Nearly all penguin species use nests. Some nest under bushes or in little caves, while others build them from scratch. A few species use the claws on their feet to create shallow holes in the ground, appropriately named "scrapes." Many penguins build nests out of lots of little stones, which can be lined with grass, moss, bones, and feathers. All nest-building penguins lay two eggs per nest.

Northern rockhopper penguins nest in tall grass.

Gentoo penguin scrape.

Adélie pebble nest.

Eggs

Penguin eggs have thick shells to protect them from breaking and a large yolk to feed the chick while it grows. Parents typically take turns to sit on the eggs to keep them warm and safe. This is known as "incubation." The other parent heads out to sea to stock up on food and may be gone for days or weeks at a time. The incubating parent simply waits without food until they return.

Chicks

When the chick is ready to hatch, it uses a special "egg tooth" at the tip of its beak to crack open the shell. Nearly all penguin chicks are covered in a thin layer of fluffy feathers that aren't yet waterproof. They are completely dependent on their parents for survival. The chick cuddles up close to one of its parents while the other goes foraging.

King penguin chicks are born without feathers.

Growing Up

For chicks to grow, they need a lot of food. A foraging parent swallows extra food and stores it in its stomach until it gets back to the nest. This can take several days. When the parent returns, it regurgitates this partially digested food into the chick's mouth in the form of a thick paste. Yes, the parent throws up in its baby's mouth! But chicks don't mind. Hungry chicks pester their parents for these easy-to-swallow snacks by tapping them on the beak. They even pester any passing adult for food, regardless of whether they know them.

This erect-crested penguin is feeding its chick. Mmm . . . delicious.

King penguin chicks lose their downy feathers to look like their parents.

Leaving the Nest

Chicks eventually grow waterproof feathers and gain enough bodyweight to start exploring the ocean. They know instinctively how to swim and hunt. For some of the smaller species, this can take only seven weeks, but large species like the king penguin are dependent on their parents for more than a year. After the chicks leave the nest, parents start their catastrophic molt.

ICE, ICE BABY

The two great penguin species both breed in the Antarctic and are the only penguins that don't build nests. King penguins stick to the beaches but emperor penguins trek up to 70 miles along sea ice to raise their chicks. Here, they experience extreme weather conditions with temperatures dropping below -40°F and cold winds reaching nearly 125 mph. This may seem like a strange place to breed, but it ensures that there are no predators around, and they don't have to compete for space with other penguin species.

Pass It On

The mother lays a single egg and gives it to the father to look after. Producing an egg takes a lot of energy, so the mother heads back to the sea to go foraging and get her strength back. Moving the egg between parents can be difficult, especially for first-time parents. Sadly, the egg is often dropped or cracked. If this happens, the relationship ends and both parents head back to the sea.

Leg Warmers

If the transfer is successful, eggs are kept in the father's "brood pouch." He balances the egg on his feet and keeps it warm against a featherless area of skin called the "brood patch." His feathery belly folds over the egg like a blanket. The brood patch senses the temperature of the egg and lets the parent know when it needs more warmth. A male emperor penguin waits in the cold for more than two months, protecting his egg. There is no food to eat here, so by the time the egg hatches, dad will have fasted for around 120 days.

*These are some seriously
dedicated parents.*

Emperor penguins shuffling into the middle of the huddle.

Huddle Up

Emperor penguins huddle together to stay warm. This way, most of the group are shielded from the constant cold and biting wind. The penguins take turns being on the outside, constantly shuffling around together so that everybody gets a turn in the middle. These tightly packed groups can contain more than 6,000 birds but they're not really touching. Contact between them would mess up their feather insulation, so they just stand very close to one another instead.

Cream of the Crop

Emperor penguin chicks usually hatch before mom comes back from her forage, so the father feeds it for around ten days using "crop milk." This thick liquid is produced within his body by a special gland. The only other birds that produce crop milk are pigeons and flamingos.

Taking Turns

The father keeps the hatched chick warm in his brood pouch. After such an intense wintery ordeal, he can often be hesitant to pass the chick over to his partner when she returns, but he needs to find food for himself. From now on, parents take turns to brood. Chicks cannot survive on their own and are totally reliant on their parents. It's very important that each parent doesn't take too long to return, otherwise the other parent will be forced to head to the sea to feed.

LOVE LIFE

Penguins pair up to raise chicks. Some partnerships are formed through bonding exercises like dancing and singing, while others are a bit more unusual, and can be based on how many rocks the male has . . . The process of selecting a mate is known as "courtship."

What Do You Look for in a Penguin?

It's hard to know exactly what penguins look for in a mate, but chubbier males often seem to be favored. Perhaps this is due to their ability to handle weeks without food while the female goes hunting. Some scientists believe that size isn't that important and it's more likely that the voice of a penguin is the deciding factor.

Dance to the Same Tune

Some courtships begin with the male showing his dance moves. If it's going well, the female will begin to mirror him. This "display" can include standing tall, bowing their heads to one another, exchanging glances, calling loudly, raising their heads to the sky, flapping outstretched wings, or following each other around a colony.

Chinstrap penguins performing a courtship dance together.

Love on the Rocks

Penguins love rocks. It's such an important nest-building material for many penguins that the sharing of these rocks is an important part of courtship. The stones are carefully protected by their owners and can be the cause of many arguments and physical fights. Penguins will often steal from their neighbors and some partnered females even respond to male courtship just to nab a good rock.

This Adélie penguin is stealing from the neighbor's nest.

Finding Love Again

Species like the emperor and king penguins stay with the same mate for one breeding season, but usually find a different partner the following year. Others, like the Magellanic penguin, tend to mate with the same partner for life. The male finds the pair's burrow from the previous year and moves back in, waiting for his partner to return. When Gentoo penguins breed with a penguin who isn't their partner, they are usually banished from the colony.

SOCIAL LIFE

Penguins are very social animals. Most live together in large colonies, known as "rookeries." Each rookery can be home to hundreds of thousands of birds but is made up of only one species of penguin. Rookeries are loud, busy, and smelly places, filled with penguins calling to each other constantly.

Give Me a Call

Penguins make many different types of noises, including trumpets, peeps, brays, whistles, and haws. Some even make two different noises at the same time. Each call type has a specific purpose. Banded penguins yell to warn others off, use donkeylike noises to impress a mate, and make soft calls known as a "throb" when a mate returns to the nest. Each penguin has a unique call, so parents, mates, and chicks can find each other even in large noisy crowds.

Take Care

As chicks grow, they spend more time away from their nest. Parents will sometimes leave chicks in a large group together, known as a "créche" while they go foraging. The chicks are looked after by other penguins in the colony.

Adélie penguins live in rookeries of up to 1.5 million individuals.

Adélie penguins often pick fights with each other.

Peck a Fight

Living so close to your neighbors can cause arguments. Penguins sometimes get into yelling matches or try to chase each other away. If they stare and point their beak, it means they want another penguin to go away. If the other penguin wants to calm the situation down, they can use a submissive "slender walk," flattening their feathers and hunching their shoulders. This shows that the first penguin has won the argument.

Throw Down

Sometimes nobody backs down. Flippers are used to hit each other and beaks are used to peck and strike their opponent. Penguins can even lock beaks together and wrestle, trying to knock the other one over.

Poo Knows

Penguin poop is known as *guano* and penguins produce a lot of it! But penguins are so used to being surrounded by poop that some even build their nests out of it. A rookery of 1.5 million Adélie penguins was once discovered because the guano stains were visible from space.

Krill are pink and Adélie penguins eat so much of them that it turns their guano (poop) a vibrant pinky-red.

LITTLE AND LARGE

Featured Creatures: Emperor Penguins

The largest species of penguin is the emperor penguin. They can reach 4 feet tall, which is about the average height of a seven-year-old human.

Featured Creatures: Little Penguins

The two smallest penguins are members of the little penguin species. Scientists only recently discovered that the populations in New Zealand and Australia were genetically different. Both species weigh the same as a 2 pound bag of sugar and are only slightly taller than a 12 inch ruler. The white-flippered subspecies of the New Zealand birds are generally the smallest of them all.

Little penguins are the only penguins that can raise more than one brood in a breeding season. Parents can sometimes raise up to three groups of eggs in a year if the conditions and weather are perfect.

Life-size adult emperor penguin

Life-size emperor penguin egg

Life-size little penguin egg

Comparison between
adult emperor penguin
and adult little penguin

Life-size adult
little penguin

TO SCALE

Small penguin species are usually found close to the equator, while larger penguins live in colder areas. Here you can see different penguins hanging out with a person.

Humboldt penguin

Little penguin

Erect-crested penguin

Chinstrap penguin

Emperor penguin

Snares penguin

Southern rockhopper penguin

King penguin

Macaroni penguin

African penguin

Yellow-eyed penguin

Fiordland penguin

Magellanic penguin

Royal penguin

Eastern rockhopper penguin

Human

Gentoo penguin

Galápagos penguin

Northern rockhopper penguin

Adélie penguin

Little penguin

4 inches

AND THE AWARD GOES TO …

Gentoo penguins sprint ahead as the fastest birds underwater. When searching for food and evading predators, they can reach speeds of 20 mph. That's more than four times faster than Olympic swimmers!

Emperor penguins can dive down more than 1,700 feet underwater. The deepest recorded dive was 1,850 feet which is about one and a half times the height of the Empire State Building in New York City. The pressure on the penguin that far down would be about 40 times more than on the surface.

Emperor penguins win a second award for holding their breath. The longest recorded dive was over 32 minutes. They have special blood which allows them to function with less oxygen. Emperor penguins can also temporarily shut down organs to conserve the oxygen in their blood.

So, which species is the grumpiest? Adélie penguins are well known for being aggressive and noisy birds, but chinstrap penguins just about win the fight. Both species sometimes nest in the same place, but Adélie penguins are bullied out of their nests by chinstrap penguins who use them for themselves.

Yellow-eyed penguins win the award for the most private penguin. Many species like to nest within large rookeries, almost within touching distance of their neighbors, but yellow-eyed penguins like to build individual nests out of sight of each other. The nests are built among plants and against trees or slopes.

Macaroni penguins strut the runway in their feathery crowns as the most fashionable penguin. These penguins are specifically named after a group of 18th-century fashionistas who wore elaborate wigs. The extravagantly dressed English "Macaronis" were themselves named after their love of Italy's macaroni pasta which was new to England at the time.

Macaroni penguin

An 18th century "Macaroni"

Macaroni pasta

33

Krill are also an important food source for humpback whales.

Melting sea ice

Commercial fishing boat

CONSERVATION

Most penguin species are becoming more endangered because of human activity.

Global Warming

One of the biggest threats to penguins is climate change. Krill are an important food source for them and they are dependent on the sea ice to breed. As Earth warms up, the sea ice in Antarctica begins to melt. This causes the amount of krill to decrease, meaning there is less food for penguins. It's thought that the number of krill in these areas is just 20% of what it was 50 years ago. Many penguins also breed on sea ice.

Overfishing

Sometimes humans overfish areas, directly reducing the amount of food available for penguins. Sections of water can be protected by law so that people can't fish there for a while. This gives the ocean a chance to regenerate and for fish and krill populations to grow . . .

Offshore oil platform

Oil Spills

When oil is extracted from the ground, transported around the world, or stored, it can sometimes spill into the ocean. Oil floats on water and can be deadly for penguins and other sea birds. Oil is poisonous when eaten and a penguin's plumage is damaged by the oil getting on their feathers.

Pipeline for oil

It is thought that more than 40,000 Magellanic penguins are killed by oil spills each year.

Oil tanker

What Can We Do?

Millions of children around the globe choose to protest for change. Governments and large companies have a lot of power to make real differences to the world around us. Governments can pass essential laws to protect breeding grounds, areas of the sea, certain species, or even guano. Companies can make big choices to use less plastic in their products, or use the earth's resources in a more sustainable way. Many people in power don't prioritize the future of animals like penguins or the habitats they live in, so maybe you can use your voice to make them listen. Educating people can be one of the most important ways to protect nature.

INDEX

Megadyptes

Eudyptes (Crested Penguins)

A group of porpoising gentoo penguins.

Collect the whole About Animals collection

To Chris, my fellow nerd.

First edition published in 2022 by Flying Eye Books Ltd.
27 Westgate Street, London, E8 3RL.

Text and illustrations © Owen Davey 2022.

Owen Davey has asserted his right under the
Copyright, Designs and Patents Act, 1988, to be identified
as the Author and Illustrator of this Work.

Scientific consultant: The Bird Department at ZSL London Zoo

Every attempt has been made to ensure any statements written as fact have been checked
to the best of our abilities. However, we are still human, thankfully, and occasionally
little mistakes may crop up. Should you spot any errors, please email info@nobrow.net.

3 5 7 9 10 8 6 4 2

Published in the US by Flying Eye Books Ltd.

Printed in Poland on FSC® certified paper.

ISBN: 978-1-83874-852-4

www.flyingeyebooks.com